Tracks in the Snow

Wong Herbert Yee

SQUARE
FISH

Henry Holt and Company

SQUARE
FISH

An Imprint of Holtzbrinck Publishers

Library of Congress Cataloging-in-Publication Data
Yee, Wong Herbert.
Tracks in the snow / Wong Herbert Yee.
Summary: A little girl investigates tracks in the snow, trying to determine what could have made them.
[1. Animal tracks—Fiction. 2. Footprints—Fiction. 3. Snow—Fiction. 4. Curiosity—Fiction. 5. Stories in rhyme.] I. Title.
PZ8.3.Y42 Tr 2003   [E]—dc21   2002010854

ISBN-13: 978-0-312-37134-0 / ISBN-10: 0-312-37134-9
Originally published in the United States by Henry Holt and Company, LLC
First Square Fish Edition: October 2007
10 9 8 7 6 5 4 3 2 1
www.squarefishbooks.com

The artist used Prismacolors on Arches watercolor paper to create the illustrations for this book.

For Ellen

Just outside my window,
There are tracks in the snow.

Who made the tracks?

Where do they go?

I skip across
The snowy yard,
Around the old oak tree.

Past the garden gate I go.
Good thing I have the key.

It's too big to be a rabbit.
No bears this time of year.

Is that a hippopotamus
Hiding over there?

Tracks in the snow.
Tracks in the snow.
Who made the tracks?
Where do they go?

In and out of rocks I squeeze,
Along a frozen pond.

Slip-slide across a snowy bridge
Into the woods beyond.

It could have been a duck,
But I think they've gone away.
I know it's not a woodchuck;
They sleep all night and day.

Tracks in the snow.
Tracks in the snow.
Who made the tracks?
Where do they go?

I peek under a fallen log,
Then tramp-stamp up a hill.
Quickly down the other side
The tracks keep going still.

Could it be a fox, a dog?
Maybe a squirrel or kitten?
Oh, look here! What's this I see?
Why, someone's lost a mitten!

Tracks in the snow.
Tracks in the snow.

Who made the tracks?
Where do they go?

My feet are getting oh so cold.
There's still no sign of *it*.
And even though the time is late,
I really hate to quit.

Snowflakes fall softly,
As quiet as a mouse.
Hey! The tracks are leading
Right back to my house.

Wait—I know who made these tracks.

I know where these tracks go . . .

I made them yesterday,
Out playing in the snow!